D0116283

WRITTEN BY **Tim McCanna**   ILLUSTRATED BY **Tad Carpenter**

BITTY BOT

A PAULA WISEMAN BOOK

Simon & Schuster Books for Young Readers · New York · London · Toronto · Sydney · New Delhi

For my adventure team:
Trudi, Nate, and Sophie—T. M.

For my mom, with love.
You are truly out of this world.—T. C.

SIMON & SCHUSTER BOOKS FOR YOUNG READERS
· An imprint of Simon & Schuster Children's Publishing
Division · 1230 Avenue of the Americas, New York,
New York 10020 · Text copyright © 2016 by Tim McCanna ·
Illustrations copyright © 2016 by Tad Carpenter · All rights
reserved, including the right of reproduction in whole or in
part in any form. · SIMON & SCHUSTER BOOKS FOR YOUNG
READERS is a trademark of Simon & Schuster, Inc. · For
information about special discounts for bulk purchases,
please contact Simon & Schuster Special Sales at 1-866-
506-1949 or business@simonandschuster.com. · The Simon
& Schuster Speakers Bureau can bring authors to your live
event. For more information or to book an event, contact
the Simon & Schuster Speakers Bureau at 1-866-248-3049
or visit our website at www.simonspeakers.com. · Book
design by Jessica Handelman · The text for this book was
set in Write Heavy. · The illustrations for this book were
rendered digitally. · Manufactured in China · 0716 SCP ·
First Edition · 10 9 8 7 6 5 4 3 2 1 · Library of
Congress Cataloging-in-Publication Data · McCanna, Tim.
Bitty Bot / Tim McCanna ; illustrated by Tad Carpenter.—
First edition. · pages cm · "A Paula Wiseman Book." ·
Summary: "All of the bots in Botsburg are powering down
for the night . . . but Bitty Bot isn't tired! Bitty decides to
build a rocket and go on a space adventure instead of going
to sleep"—Provided by publisher. · ISBN 978-1-4814-4929-8
(hardcover)—ISBN 978-1-4814-4930-4 (eBook) · [1. Stories
in rhyme. 2. Bedtime—Fiction. 3. Robots—Fiction. 4. Space
flight to the moon—Fiction.] I. Carpenter, Tad, illustrator.
II. Title. · PZ8.3.M13193Bi 2016 · [E]—dc23 · 2014049992

all except for Bitty Bot.
Feeling sleepy? Maybe not.

All the bots in Botsburg beep:
"Day is over. Time for sleep!"

"Kiss your papas, hug your mamas.
Activate your bot pajamas."

Every bot is tucked in tight?
Peace and quiet?

Well . . . not quite.

What's that noise in tower three?
Who in Botsburg could it be?

Bitty Bot with power tools!
Breaking all the bedtime rules.

Banging bolts and
welding wings.

Clanging cogs and tubes and springs.

BONK!

"At last! My work is done.

Start the countdown.

Three...

two...

one!"

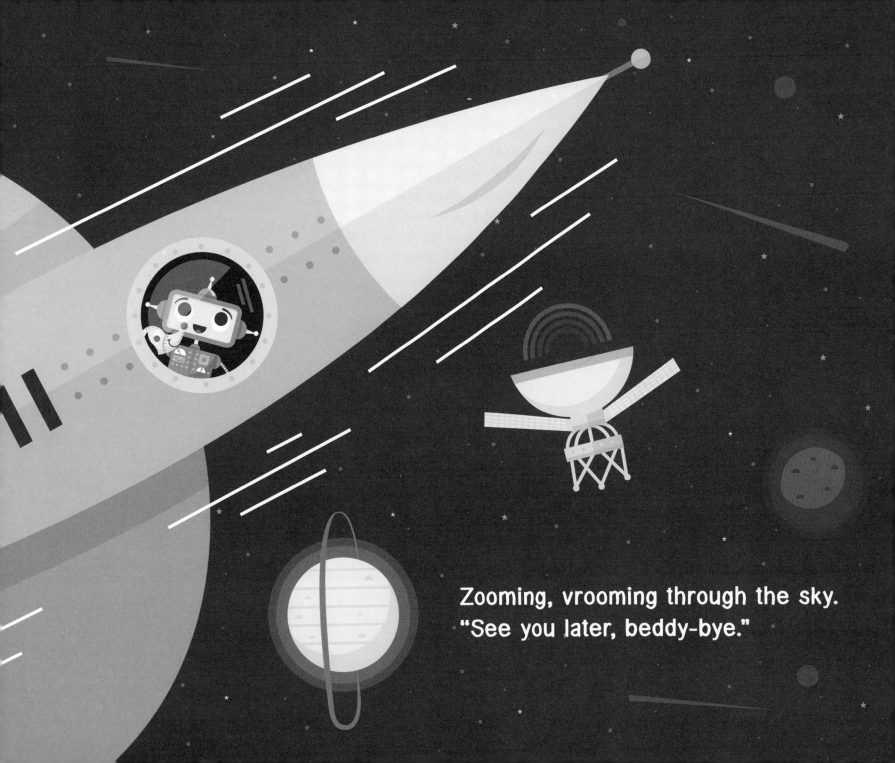

Zooming, vrooming through the sky.
"See you later, beddy-bye."

Touching down, and pretty soon,
Bitty Bot is on the moon.

Taking in the sights to see—
"Oops! Hello there. Pardon me."

Bitty bounces left and right.
Jumping, bumping through the night.

As the party lingers on,
Bitty Bot begins to yawn.

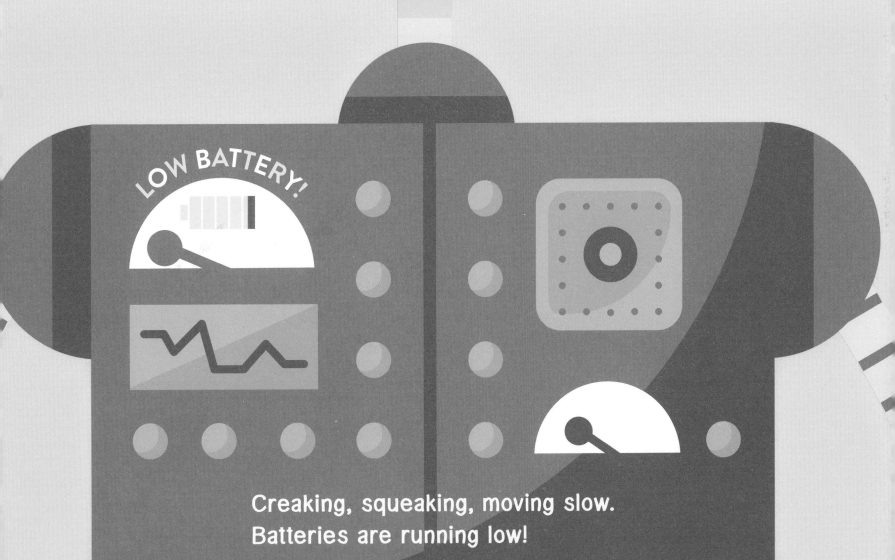

LOW BATTERY!

Creaking, squeaking, moving slow.
Batteries are running low!

Hurry, Bitty! Back to bed!
You should be at home instead.

Rockets rumble. Boosters blast.
Bitty Bot is fading fast.

Systems shutting off, unless—

Almost . . .

nearly . . .

maybe . . .

yes!

Safely home and done exploring.
Sound asleep and softly snoring.

DING! Good morning! Robots, rise!
Time for bots to mobilize.

Bright and shiny. On the dot.

All except for Bitty Bot!